Poems of Love,Loss and Longing

The Moon Didn't Wait for you Either

MUBASHIRA VAKAYIL

BlueRose ONE .com
Stories Matter
NewDelhi • London

BLUEROSE PUBLISHERS
India | U.K.

BlueRose ONE.com
Stories Matter
NewDelhi • London

For permissions requests or inquiries regarding this publication, please contact:

BLUEROSE PUBLISHERS
www.BlueRoseONE.com
info@bluerosepublishers.com
+91 8882 898 898
+4407342408967

ISBN: 978-93-7139-140-5

Cover design: Yash Singhal
Typesetting: Namrata Saini

First Edition: October 2025

PREFACE

This book is a pilgrimage—through love's cathedral halls, through grief's barren landscapes, through silence that echoes like prayer, and back to the altar of self.

Each poem on these pages carries a pulse. Some are fragments of memory crystallized into verse, others woven from yearning and the gossamer threads of vision. Many arise from the sacred, hidden chambers of a woman's spirit—where love bloomed like night jasmine, where pain was endured in hushed reverence, and where healing took root slowly, deliberately, like moonlight learning to trust the dark.

These are not indictments carved in stone.

These are not revelations proclaimed from mountaintops.

They are echoes of emotion made manifest. Moments captured in metaphor's amber light. Truths that breathe in feeling's cathedral, not in fact's cold chapel.

This collection maps the geography of transformation—Eight phases like lunar stations, each one a different country of the heart. Here, you will find the hollow sky of waiting, the tender bloom of first love, the full burn of believing in forever, and the pale rise of a woman who learned that healing sounds like her own voice, singing in the night.

Read these pages as you would watch the moon—with patience, with wonder, and with the understanding that even in its waning, it never truly disappears.

It only learns, in Twilight, how to rise again.

DISCLAIMER

This collection dwells in the realm of creative interpretation—where memory dances with imagination, and emotional truth transcends literal fact. While these verses may echo the author's lived experience, they are not intended as documentary testimony of specific individuals, circumstances, or connections.

Names have been transformed, timelines have been reimagined, and events have been alchemized through the crucible of artistic expression. Any resemblance to actual persons, living or departed, exists purely in the realm of coincidence.

These poems are not accusations hurled like stones, nor claims seeking legal remedy. They do not seek to wound or diminish, but rather to illuminate the shadowed corners of human experience that often remain voiceless.

This work stands as testament to emotional landscapes—the geography of a heart learning to navigate love, loss, betrayal, and ultimately, the fierce geography of healing. It speaks for those who have loved deeply, lost quietly, and risen anyway.

In poetry, we seek not absolute truth, but truth that resonates–the kind that makes us nod in recognition, not in litigation.

DEDICATION

To the love that once cradled me like dawn and the silence that followed like winter's longest night–
Not to mourn what crumbled into dust, but to honour what phoenix-rose from those ashes.
In the ruins, I discovered my fire.
In losing you, I unearthed my voice.
In learning to let go, I found my way home–to myself.

INTRODUCTION
"BEFORE THE FIRST POEM"

There was a girl who believed love could mend anything.
She gave, waited, wept, and bloomed—again and again.
She gave, stayed open, grieved, and flourished—time after time.
Not because someone remained,
but because, even when abandoned,
she still chose to feel.
This is not a plea for sympathy.
It is not a letter seeking resolution.
It is not retaliation disguised as verse.
This is a collection of my becoming.
Of the yearning I carried in silence,
and the poetry that rose from it.
I stood beneath countless skies.
I whispered to moons that refused to answer.
But in the end,
I became my own dawn.
These poems are pages of a woman
who loved fearlessly,
broke quietly,
and stitched herself whole, word by word.
If you've ever lingered for a presence
that never turned the key—
these pages belong to you too.

PHASES

1. Hollow Sky *(The Waiting)*

An empty night aching for stars.

2. New Bloom *(The Beginning)*

The first tender spark of connection, delicate and untouched.

3. Waxing *(The Becoming)*

A slow ascent in silver arcs—uncertain, rising.

4. Full Burn *(The Peak)*

Radiance at its fiercest—complete, fragile, blazing.

5. Waning *(The Unravelling)*

The gradual dimming of what once felt eternal.

6. Eclipse *(The End)*

What once shimmered now fades—gentle, dissolving.

7. Pale Rise *(The Rebirth)*

Luminescence returns—thinner, wiser. So do you.

8. Blood Moon *(The Reveal)*

The truth spills red into the night—exposing what hid in shadow.

CONTENTS

Phase 1: Hollow Sky (The Waiting)

Before you had a name,
you were already the silence between constellations.
I lived beneath a sky without moon–
vast, expectant, unanswered.
These are the poems from the time I reached
toward the outline of you in the shadow,
not knowing I was already in love
with the ache of your arrival.

Sky Without Moon

There was a time before you,
but it drifted—hollow, untouched.
Days heavy with the weight of existing,
nights threaded with sorrow
no one dared unravel.

I was the girl cast aside by her own blood,
haunted by questions that prowled like winter wolves
where a father's voice should have echoed.
I watched my sister fade from this world,
a wisp in the morning air,
and no one showed me how to mourn
what never returns.

My mother—
part woman, part battlefield—
held my fragments together with prayer-worn hands
and devotion that never asked for anything back.

I grew up aching—
not for safety,
but to be recognized.
For someone to look at the tempest in me
and stay.

I etched affection on unfamiliar faces,
folded it into unsent letters,
laid it in the arms of dreams
that vanished with the dawn.
I craved something deeper than rescue.

Not to be saved–
to be chosen.
Held in a way that felt whole, not borrowed.

This is where I was–
beneath a sky stripped of its moon,
speaking to wind,
naming stars after a future
I couldn't fully believe would come.
From the moment I adored a presence I couldn't
name–
whispering to phantoms,
unaware I was already in love
with a longing
that wore your face in my dreams.

The Unnamed Longing

I carried you
before I knew how to name that kind of yearning.
Before your face held form,
you moved in the pause between heartbeats–
a half-formed prayer
I only whispered when the world looked away.

I wrote letters
addressed to no one,
folded them around the corners of hope,
and placed them in drawers
heavy with expectation.

You settled in the stillness
when everything around me blurred.
The breath I held
passing someone who nearly mirrored you.
A presence with no place to return.

In cafés thick with voices, on rain-slick streets,
I gripped a belief–
knotted, fraying,
some fragile thread
that dared to believe you existed.

No hand reached for mine by nightfall.
But I loved as if you'd already arrived,
as if each empty chair
belonged to your absence.

They said affection wasn't built
for girls raised on fault lines—
where men didn't stay,
and tenderness wasn't plated in gold.
But I'd seen devotion grow
in the cracks no one tended.

At twenty-three,
I moved through a city of colour
with grey sewn into my steps.
They didn't see me—
but I was full of you.
The voice I imagined
would sound like home,
the nearness that could one day
echo the ache.

And maybe that was enough—
to believe in someone
not yet part of my mornings,
but already curled
inside the unspoken rooms of my heart.

The Shape of You in the Dark

I never glimpsed your face,
only sensed your luminescence–
not as someone who arrived with fanfare,
but as someone who lingered
when silence demanded solitude.

You materialized in my most buried hours–
a weightless constellation,
a solace I never grasped
yet somehow harboured.

Certain evenings, I turned toward obsidian depths
and conjured your embrace–
not cradling my flesh,
but anchoring the melancholy
that surged without herald.
You moved with reverence.

A man who didn't amplify his voice
to command attention.
Someone who encountered my anguish
and didn't retreat.
I wasn't seeking perfection.

Only someone
who would witness me and abide.
Who wouldn't recoil from the vastness I carried,
or calibrate my worth
by what I abandoned.

Perhaps you were a reverie stitched from yearning–
but I cherished you as if you were sinew,
as if your footfalls
were approaching the threshold
of a life awaiting communion.

The moon, in her phases,
knew this longing–
how we orbit around emptiness,
pulling at tides of hope
until something solid
finally emerges from shadow.

Listening for Footsteps

I encountered multitudes.
Exchanged whispered syllables with strangers
who solicited treasures they hadn't earned.
They smiled, but their gazes thundered.

Some draped allure like cologne,
yet their phrases carved welts.
Others tarried beyond welcome,
and I mistook inertia for sanctuary—
until pain transformed to blade
and I recalled
how isolation deepens beside the erroneous
companion.
I attended.
With lunar precision.
For a cadence that wouldn't distort my compassion
into something diminished.

Yet all I perceived were reverberations
of what I declined to beckon.
Initial dialogues shrouded in enigmas.
Mirth acrid with theatrics.
Inquiries threaded with possession,
responses spiralling toward void.

Still,
I persevered.
I excavated every crevice of dawn,
as though presence might unfurl from a glimpse,
as though devotion could surface
from the susurrus before utterance.

Even zephyrs caressing my flesh
seemed to ferry you—
a whisper of resonance, an essence,
an intuition too ethereal to articulate.
And I inquired,
Is it you this time?
But I perpetually discerned.
Each instance,
I discerned.

You were never bewilderment.
Never pedagogy.
Not sport.
You were the serenity still approaching.
And I was attending—
for footfalls that pulsed like homecoming.

The Room I Made for You

I ceased pursuing phantoms
and christening hollow vessels with your essence.
Yet I never relinquished the yearning–
not entirely.

I craved devotion that cradled me
without submerging me within its depths.
Fingers that would seek mine
without questioning excess.
A torso to recline against
when my universe tilted toward chaos.
Hands to draw coverlets close–
not from solicitation,
but from intrinsic worth.

So–
I cultivated sanctuary.
I burnished the harsh contours of my aloneness.
Preserved one hemisphere of the mattress pristine,
as though radiance might navigate there.

I murmured to obsidian hours
as if they might courier tidings of me to you.
I didn't supplicate the constellations,
yet I gazed skyward nonetheless–
trusting they'd illuminate the trajectory.

This was never capitulation.
Never genuflection in anticipation.
It was adoration preceding form.
Forbearance worn intimate,
like epidermis.

And should you materialize—
should your passage ever guide you here—
I won't interrogate your origins.
I'll merely declare:
this is the chamber I architected for you.
And I sustained conviction
that you'd navigate toward its threshold.
Like the moon preparing her crescent bower
for the sun's eventual return,
I made myself ready
for a love not yet born.

Phase 2: New Bloom (The Beginning)

You arrived as a season I hadn't yet lived–
warm, unfolding, quietly certain.
I knew you,
as if my heart had been whispering your presence for years.
These poems unfurl from that first gentle hour–
when love felt like sunlight falling through a window,
and I finally pulled the curtains back
to let the light touch everything.

The Night the Wind Whispered Your Name

Before your voice traversed the distance,
I was already attuned–
to breezes that bore no missives,
to hushed pauses too gravid to contain.

You materialized not as destiny, but as benediction–
unwavering and corporeal.
A tender advent
from one who still deemed me
deserving of genesis.

I dialled with trembling digits,
unknowing I was unfastening a portal
I'd been petitioning for epochs.
Your timbre was ephemeral–
gentle, nearly vanished,
a solitary ember amid tempest.
Yet it lingered.

It wove through temporal chasms
for forty-eight protracted hours
until you beckoned again–
and the cosmos pivoted.
Within your syllables,
I discovered tranquility I'd never inhabited.
A soul who didn't saturate atmosphere
merely to sense his own resonance.

No vows.
No orchestration.
Only existence—
contemplative and unhurried,
as though you'd encountered devastation
and elected not to transmit its poison.
And I,
a woman nurtured on vigilance,
retreated into shadow
and breathed toward whatever attended:
"Let this manifest as truth."
Because I had commenced descending—
not from vacancy,
but from the measured, intentional euphoria
of being encountered
without dissolution.

The crescent moon witnessed this moment,
how a single voice
could shift the entire night sky
from hollow to luminous.

The Unspoken Covenant

You hadn't uttered the syllables,
yet I had begun interpreting–
not your declarations,
but what your proximity ignited
in the hollowed intervals between.

You promised nothing.
Still, I knelt as though paradise
had pooled within my cupped hands.
I carried countless minute mortifications,
stitched from rebuff,
interlaced with vacancy–
a woman from fractured foundations,
schooled to murmur softly
lest she commandeer too much air.

You remained unaware
of my quivering as I answered your calls.
How each dialogue felt stolen–
a fragment I feared
might slip through my grasp.

You embodied composure,
dispensing affection
as though it belonged to every creature.
You absorbed, and I...
I flourished, solely from that gift.

My intellect whispered warnings—
that men wielding compassion
don't tarry for women forged by grief.
Yet my heart harboured its own dialect,
already declining your name
through devotion I couldn't abandon.
I composed stanzas never transmitted,
simply to inhabit your memory.

Revealed those I could,
starving for your spoken touch.
You never declared permanence.
But within those initial muted conversations,
you granted something rarer—
justification to believe
that even someone marked by wounds
was entitled to yearn
for something radiant.

The crescent moon comprehended this ache—
how affection manifests not through oaths
but in the chambers where
two spirits synchronize their heartbeats.

The Hue That Haunts My Reveries

I beheld you initially in suspension—
not amid movement, not within clamor,
but captured within an image
that contained more authenticity
than any instant I had inhabited.

You donned a coral-salmon garment,
a twilight-saturated pigment
that curved toward closure
without surrendering its mystery.

That tint pursues me perpetually—
fervent, evanescent,
something exquisite I feared to graze.
You displayed no grin.
You weren't soliciting observation.
Perhaps that's what dismantled me—
how you pivoted from the aperture,
a soul with nothing to validate,
yet somehow, everything to bestow.

I gazed as though it bore significance—
as if the fold in your neckline
or how your scrutiny departed the border
could articulate the burden I shouldered
eons before your emergence.

You never extended a covenant.
Yet I discovered refuge
in the fortitude of your motionlessness,
in how you mirrored intermission
rather than exhibition.
You resonated like an inception
that required no vindication.

And I–
a maiden shattered by her own mirage,
uncertain she'd ever suffice–
positioned herself for the premiere time
within the prospect
that someone might perceive her
without solicitation.

Thus I beseeched.
Not for fantasies.
But for the hushed opportunity
to be fathomed by someone
who wouldn't attempt reconstruction first.

It remained merely a photograph,
a motionless tableau in a mutable cosmos.
Yet that dawn,
my pulse acknowledged something.

That dawn,
I permitted it to gravitate toward you.
The gibbous moon witnessed this moment—
how a single captured second
could rewrite the entire constellation
of what the heart dares to hope.

All the Radiance Before Your Arrival

The universe murmured,
"The hour has arrived."
Not through tempest,
but via tranquility forged from conviction t
hat flowed within me like dawn's inaugural caress.

When you declared our encounter imminent,
something molten unfurled beneath my ribs—
the exhilaration of being selected,
not within some remote possibility,
but imminently.

This transcended ordinary rendezvous.
It signified a gateway.
A clandestine commencement between
two souls that had extensively wandered
toward one another,
oblivious to the distances.

I navigated through hours
as though summoned by someone
who honored every utterance.

The firmament appeared more profound.
My gait more anchored.
Tomorrow, mellower along its periphery.

I nurtured a grin below the surface–
an awareness, as though
existence had finally acknowledged my direction.

For once, I wasn't maintaining the portal for affection
while wishing it would elect to cross.
It had discovered its passage inward.

Your vow to converge wasn't merely notation upon parchment–
it became the opening fiber
woven into a narrative I had solely envisioned.

Even preceding my entrance into that occasion,
before gazes connected,
before voices traversed the chasm separating us,
I already blazed internally
from the fever of approaching destiny.

And within that instant,
the heaviness I bore diminished.
No recesses remained barren.

I possessed orientation.
I possessed illumination.
And for the inaugural time in countless seasons,
I trusted I was advancing toward devotion—
not retreating from it.

The waning moon observed this transformation,
understanding how anticipation can kindle
the spirit long before
two hearts discover their shared rhythm.

You Arrived Without Armor

You didn't attempt to dazzle me.
No pilfered verses,
no burnished veneer.
Only yourself–vulnerable, rooted,
the species of veracity I had craved
to encounter in motionless atmosphere.

When I crossed that threshold,
my sternum constricted–
not with anxiety, but recognition.
Somehow, I understood my essence
had been positioned precisely where you dwelled.

We occupied opposing spaces,
but our vision collapsed the expanse.
No pledges.
No rehearsed tomorrows.
Only existence–stable and authentic,
a haven I needn't purchase.

And then the journey–
solely us and the deluge,
advancing leisurely through
a realm that suddenly felt consecrated.

You activated the melody,
the one I still harbor note by note,
as though every verse had waited
for this moment to breathe.

We didn't articulate extensively,
but the void between us cradled
elements that required no expression.

You absorbed completely.
You responded with deliberation.
You permitted me to flourish—
every fragment of me.

And I, who had perpetually compressed myself
minute to nestle into palms
that never lingered, began to expand.

Somewhere between precipitation and euphoria,
you bestowed a WATCH.
A pristine gesture—calculated, purposeful.
You didn't elaborate it. You needn't.

You had already contributed duration,
manifestation, and a genesis
I never trusted I'd attain.

That afternoon, I didn't fracture for the offering.
I blossomed because you persisted—
not masquerading, not requesting me to vanish.

And if affection ever communicates
without requiring language,
it did that afternoon—in the downpour,
in your intonation, in the comprehension
we both sheltered in stillness.

The full moon bore witness to this sacred meeting—
how two souls can recognize their completion
in the space of a single glance,
a shared silence,
a gift given without expectation.

Phase 3: Waxing (The Becoming)

You were the silver edge of a growing moon–
soft, sure, and drawing me near.
We were learning the contours of each other,
gradually settling beneath the same light.
These poems rise from the quiet beginning again,
where love wasn't only felt–
it was built,
through every shared glance, every wordless room,
and the promise that distance
would not unmake what we were becoming.

The Day Luna Suspended Her Arc

It surpassed fantasy–
not constructed from vapor or remoteness,
but tangible, earthbound, incandescent.
And you were positioned at the epicentre of it.
Not within fiction,
but in a chamber perfumed with jasmine and
jubilation.

I observed the universe dissolve–
companions, blossoms, the burst of lenses–
but you remained crystalline, unwavering,
a force I needn't interrogate.

I clasped your fingers as though
I were stabilizing an entire existence,
and in that instant, I realized:
this is how eternity commences.
Not with clamor,
but with tenderness reflected in my mother's beam
and the gentle certainty in her gaze that declared,
"You selected wisely."

I yearned to halt chronology,
gather everyone proximate, and announce,
"This is the gentleman I beseeched the heavens for."

The illumination, the harmonies,
the cuisine I scarcely sampled–
all of it receded behind your voice
addressing me as though
every syllable was hallowed.

And when we positioned ourselves together–
two unwavering pulses amid
a multitude assembled to commemorate–
I finally grasped what it signifies to reach sanctuary.

That day, the moon didn't ascend.
She lingered–merely to observe us transform
into what even celestial bodies dare to covet.

The new moon held her breath that day–
understanding that some unions are so profound,
even the cosmos must pause to honor their beginning.

The Architecture of Eternity

There existed no manuscript
for the devotion we discovered–
only the whisper of acceptance
warming gradually within our grasp.

Only you, only me,
learning how to declare "I belong to you"
with no utterances whatsoever.

Your caress reached
the territories within me
that never realized they were anticipating.

This wasn't appetite–
it was a homecoming,
an encounter more ancient than recollection.

Every stroke of your digits
bore significance I didn't solicit–
not articulated, not vowed, but present–
the way twilight comprehends darkness
without questioning why, it approaches.

My flesh adapted to your proximity.
Your attendance at my shoulder
resembled dawn filtering through
apertures sealed too extensively.

We progressed deliberately.
We materialized. Repeatedly–
through feelings, through amazement,
in a hush that didn't petition to be identified.

Adoration appeared thus:
your stare constant in the dim radiance,
your palm in mine–
not extending but already positioned.

That evening, we transcended anatomy.
We became confidence made manifest–
a serene assurance shared through contact,
where two spirits needn't vocalize to communicate,
remain.

The half-moon watched over this sacred union–
recognizing that some intimacies are written
in the language of skin and souls,
where forever is measured not in time
but in the depth of two hearts choosing
to surrender completely.

The Most Fervent Frost

I arrived to you as climate transforming–
bearing all my contained yearning,
magnetized by the hushed gravity of your realm.
Not permanently, but for days
that unfolded like something extensively overdue.

In your metropolis,
through uncharted boulevards,
your vicinity was the sole location
I felt completely fathomed.

You welcomed me with vision
that identified mine through instinct–
with solicitude that never requested acknowledgment,
but enveloped itself around me regardless.

We occupied rented chambers,
your intonation revealing the sunrise
with a stability that calmed me.
You cultivated warmth in porcelain,
and I consumed it leisurely,
attempting not to forfeit a singular moment.

The atmosphere beyond was trembling,
but our merriment spiralled through the recesses
like flames we never needed to kindle.
Your timbre softened the barriers,

transformed every interval into nectar—
unhurried, aureate, and cascading
tenderly into the void separating us.

On that summit,
with Horsley gusts pursuing our expressions,
I abandoned how to shield myself.
The heavens were expansive,
but your closeness was what anchored the universe.

That evening wasn't crafted from tapers or confection.
It was your limb across my clavicle,
your nearness rooting me while your gaze declared,
"This holds weight. Absorb this."
And I did. I continue to.

When I left,
your fragrance lingered in my fabric,
your quietude merged into mine.
Even the farewell couldn't freeze me—
not when I had discovered
how affection could thaw the most glacial periods
into a variety of renaissance
I didn't know I could access.

The gibbous moon illuminated this precious
interlude—
understanding how brief encounters
can plant seeds of warmth that bloom
long after the season has passed.

In All the Miles Between Us

We entered love the way sunrise
discovers the heavens–silent,
expanding, intact.
And then, we began stirring in distinct chambers,
inhabiting days in settlements
where intimacy had to traverse extended hours
and spans that could not be connected by language.

I learned to carry you in the intervals of my day–
between weary mornings and corridor radiance,
in the aroma of brew that no longer bore your chuckle.

I wasn't dwelling.
Only positioned in a location
that yearned for your touch,
yearned for the way your tone used to calm the dusk.

Evenings were the most challenging–
not solitary but lacking something whole.
Your void made even starlight retreat.
The mattress never truly disturbed.
The atmosphere never completely heated.

But then–you materialized.
In methods I didn't anticipate.
A gentle tap, a grin fracturing open the day
the way sunlight divides dense vapor.

We watched our first movie together—
not for the story,
but for the miracle,
for the wonder of simply resting
near with no gap tugging at the edges.

Every journey became a recollection.
Portals lowered. Spirits accessible.
The current softened itself when you were close,
your palm discovering mine as if it had never departed.

Affection didn't diminish.
It intensified—in the anticipation,
in the craving, in calculating the rotations
until I'd perceive your features again.

And even separated,
you discovered methods to restore the realm to me.
With presence alone,
you reminded me that the expanse between us
had only ever been a pathway leading sanctuary.

The waning crescent moon understood
this ache of separation—
how love learns to exist in the spaces between
presence,
growing stronger with each reunion,
each return to wholeness.

The Quarantine Luna

We traversed through luminous leagues,
your grip firm upon the controls,
my pulse unpacking
into a sanctuary we hadn't reached yet.

No vows journeyed with us–
only expanding optimism that
these brief periods might evolve
into an instant we'd transport onward.

Your dwelling awaited–
sparse, cozy, nothing but a mobile mattress,
several implements, and the exhilaration of
commencing.
 No opulence,
no magnificence–only us.
And oh, what a cosmos that was.

Three rotations in,
the planet halted–isolation proclaimed.
No locomotives, no vehicles, no reversing.
And suddenly, we were granted
what we didn't realize we'd required:
Time, tranquility, and
the bliss of awakening to each other's countenances.

No visitors, no clamor, no disruptions.

You and I became sunrise and dusk,
brilliance and shade, routine and astonishment.

We prepared with what we possessed,
consumed upon the surface,
and chuckled as though it was more than adequate.

I had only two garments—
the remainder abandoned in another settlement.
So your tunics became my shelter,
and your embrace, my mooring.

I was indisposed for a rotation,
and you remained proximate—
your hushed attendance declaring
all the concern I had never solicited.

Confined within four humble boundaries,
we discovered our inaugural dwelling—
not constructed of stone,
not purchased with earnings,
but fashioned from available chronology,
modest nourishment,
and the gradual cadence of learning
to cherish with no diversions.
It wasn't the world we planned.
It was something better.
The waxing moon sealed us within those walls—
creating a cocoon where love could grow
undisturbed, unhurried, unobserved
by the world outside.

Phase 4: Full Burn (The Peak)

You rose in me like a full moon–
bright, unblinking, and whole.
These are the poems from the nights
when love burned without hesitation,
when our hearts spoke in a language
only the dark could hear.
No more shadows, no more waiting–
just the quiet fire of two souls
Finally, fully ablaze.

You Were Always the Destination

We compressed our existence into pliant satchels–
borrowed garments, cleansed containers,
euphoria still adhering to our surfaces
like mist on glass.

After seasons of stirring beside your visage–
two brushes in one cracked vessel,
two spirits mastering how to exist
beneath one canopy–we returned.

Back to our birthplace.
Back to the pathways
that once knew us individually.

Then arrived the intermission.
Fifteen rotations of separated firmament.
You on one edge of the township,
me on the opposite–not remote,
but inaccessible,
held apart by precaution, and minutes dragging past
us.

I longed for your stillness as much as your utterance.

In those periods,
every item surrounding me felt incorrect.
I consumed, but didn't savor.

I slumbered, but repose never arrived.
How do you rest without the warmth beside you
that reminds you're secure.

But then–you returned.
With your kindred, your recognized territories,
and all the hushed delights that emerge
when you are no longer touring someone's existence,
but genuinely within it.

Then arrived Munnar–
our inaugural escape as partners.
Twisting peaks slowed
their respiration to permit us passage.

Your palm on the mechanism,
mine beyond the opening,
capturing breeze and marvel.

The passages curved like inquiries,
and your beam kept responding to them.

We halted when the precipitation requested us to,
nourished when affection beckoned us–
a roadside beverage,
a heated dish between our knees,
melodies playing softly,
your fingers caressing mine
like a custom made fresh again.

Not even haze could obscure what we had initiated.

I didn't require a chart.
I required your intonation, your vicinity,
your observation in dawn illumination—
the method you regarded me not as a terminus,
but as the route you were pleased to traverse.

Those periods were fleeting.
But they were complete.
Complete as a captured instant,
complete as a glance that persists,
complete in the manner devotion sometimes is—
unmeasured, and still more than sufficient.

The crescent moon traced our mountain journey—
understanding that some paths lead not to places,
but to the discovery of who
we become when we travel them together.

Where Love Takes Root

We arrived with hearts still tender from farewell,
stepping into rooms that held no memory of us–
yet waited, patient as dawn,
to be claimed.
Your fresh beginning. Our emerging rhythm.

A skyline we hadn't learned by heart,
though already it whispered of belonging–
because you breathed beside me.
We required so little: mornings bathed in amber light,
evenings dissolving into each other's warmth,
limbs heavy from the day's labor,
yet souls stretched wide as sky.

We discovered the city through glass and wonder,
tracing new pathways, mapping unfamiliar corners–
not merely inhabiting this space,
but weaving the life we dared to dream.

Some dawns arrived like benedictions.
Others bore the gravity of storms.
Yet even in the smallest rituals–
shared bread, your voice threading through silence,
my fingers seeking yours across darkness–
something enduring took hold.
Love entered not with fanfare
but like seasons changing:

in sunbeams painting our walls golden,
in how we honored each other's chaos,
each other's stillness,
each other's truth.

No more hesitation. No more doubt's sharp whisper.
Only this: breathing. Blooming.
And in every threshold of our sanctuary,
love made itself at home–
unhurried, wordless,
woven into all we no longer
needed to defend.

Our Everyday, Our Everything

What began as whispered phone calls through midnight
now rests solid in our ordinary—
constant, certain, close.
We crafted this without grand gestures.
Instead: your palm finding mine in slumber,
my skin memorizing the heft of your exhaustion
in languages that need no translation.

Adventures unfolded on forgotten highways—
wandering, boundless, our joy spilling
across empty asphalt as though
darkness had carved out sanctuary for two.

We tasted new places
in shared bites,
spilled stories into recipes that fell apart
and still filled us.

The couch witnessed iterations of us
no photograph could capture—
screen casting blue shadows,
your temple against my thigh,
my fingers writing slow love letters
through the knots in your hair
my touch tracing slow poetry

through tangles you never needed to explain,
deciphering secrets your silence freely offered.

When drowsiness arrived, we gravitated inward.
Your warmth pressed to mine,
our bodies arcing toward each other
as if mattress springs could archive
this precise geometry of devotion.

When you travelled,
I counted the silence in rooms you once filled.
I left a space at the table,
in the sheets,
in the stillness held between one moment and the next.

We didn't just live.
We belonged–
to a home stitched with devotion,
to a life unfolding beneath our hands,
to each other,
so entirely
that even silence felt like saying
"I love you."

Even the Sky Looked Our Way

Time flowed like honey, and we moved with it–
not escaping affection, but diving deeper
into its currents.
Each dawn brought ritual kisses.
Each dusk, ceremonies that spelled sanctuary.

We weren't hunting tomorrow–
we were already breathing inside it.
With every fresh chapter,
we evolved too–
toward better positions, confident fingers,
a truer draft of the connection
we'd first sketched from fragments and proximity.
We purchased possibility, not merely structure.

A destiny carved by dual signatures,
and stationed beneath it–
your euphoria on wheels:
obsidian, fierce,
that Volkswagen radiating
your brand of triumph.

It hadn't been my vision.
Yet the light in your face
proved reason enough
to claim it as shared territory.

Expense became irrelevant—
not when your elation transformed
every journey into festival.

Not when evening breeze carried proof
of how seamlessly we inhabited
this existence we'd sculpted
with weathered hands and receptive spirits.
Observers declared us flawless.
Some with wonder, others with suspicion.

Occasionally, I worried
even storms might covet
our sense of place.
Still, we pressed forward—
glass down, your mirth
the singular navigation I required.

And throughout everything—
upholstery, amber streetlight,
your palm hovering near the shifter—
one thought persisted:
I would select this existence
endlessly, simply to witness
you are inhabiting what you'd once
only dreamed, with me alongside,
understanding completely—
it was always ours to discover.

In All the Ways, I Loved You

I loved you
in the golden hours–
those unhurried, hallowed dawns
when your warmth lingered near mine,
and existence held its breath
in the cathedral of our space.

I Loved you
in rising vapor and filtered rays,
in the euphoria of synchronized patterns,
in glances exchanged
across granite surfaces
beyond the reach of language.

I loved you
when joy reverberated
through sun-drunk corridors,
when your skin discovered mine
in twilight's tender grip.
Even stillness brimmed
with your proximity.

I awaited you
like tides await the pull–
relentless, faithful.
And upon your arrival,
every chamber in my chest
burst wide.

I loved you
in correspondence never delivered,
in dishes seasoned with your preferences,
in melodies that echoed your gaze,
in countless subtleties
invisible to others,
yet crystal to you.

Each instant beside you
felt like silk
spun into eternity's tapestry.
I catalogued the architecture of your fingers,
the percussion of metal against wood,
the way you spoke my name
like sanctuary incarnate.

You were my fortress,
my haven,
the quiet rhythm
that orchestrated existence.

I was never more authentic
than in the act of cherishing you.

And within that devotion–
crystalline, unwavering, softly luminous–
I discovered rapture
requiring no translation,
only witness.

Phase 5: Waning (The Unravelling)

Once, we were all light–
certain, whole, untouchable.
But the moon must turn away,
and in that gentle dimming,
love began to flicker.
These are the poems from when the glow softened–
when voices bent,
shadows lengthened,
and I learned that even in love,
the sky can lie.

The Space That Grew Between Us

I once trusted emptiness could cradle tenderness–
a peace suspended between two synchronized souls,
where closeness required no translation.

But now,
your stillness carries frost.
Not solace,
but separation
erected between us
like a sealed threshold.

You once delighted
in life's minutiae–
how I prepared your morning brew,
the rasp of my voice
piercing dawn's veil.
Now, even kindness
feels precarious,
ready to shatter.

I inquire about your hours,
yet your responses
dissolve like smoke–
drifting toward territories
beyond my reach.

Still,
you offer fragments
of our former constellation:
fingers against my spine,

whispered contrition,
a look
that nearly resurrects yesterday.
Sufficient to sustain hope.
Sufficient to mask the ache.

You invoke "we,"
speak of mutual selections,
of verdicts reached in harmony–
yet the path we traverse
echoes solely
with your rhythm.

I used to think
love was a daily vow,
a choosing
again and again.
Now I wonder
when you stopped choosing me–
but why my heart
refuses to follow

A Love Measured in Crumbs

I once trusted
that fractured affection
remained affection—
that fleeting gestures
might accumulate
into permanence.
So I survived on offerings,
graciously,
as parched earth
welcomes the briefest downpour.
A touch sustained,
gentle syllables—
I collected them all
like fallen stars
from a tempest.
You became my universe.
Not from emptiness,
but from deliberate selection
with every fiber of my being.
No refuge existed for my weariness,
no counsel echoing
instructions for survival—
only your voice,
and I obeyed.

So I yielded.
Softly, perpetually.
When our sanctuary
transformed into public theater,
when the hush of our private cosmos
shattered
beneath intrusive gazes
and judgments
that entered without invitation.

Yet I radiated joy.
Yet I offered generosity.
I extended comfort
where none was requested,
treasures wrapped in velvet
to palms that never comprehended
what it required
simply to preserve compassion.

Even emptiness,
even motionlessness,
exceeded acceptable limits.

And when I grasped
for something minor–
an hour with my mother,
oxygen for my lungs–
even that was measured
as though it disturbed equilibrium
I'd never consented to maintain.

Yet I remained anchored.
Not from weakness,
but from faith–
with the hushed dedication
only devotion can inspire–
that perhaps,
if I surrendered sufficient pieces,
you might eventually
return to me complete.

The Apology I Carried

You summoned me–
though I whispered,
my arms were laden,
my flesh worn
from cycles that refused conclusion.
But certain forms of devotion
don't demand–
they compress.

A hushed insistence
masquerading as freedom
yet never truly optional.
You declared,
"Either now or never."

So I performed my ritual–
contracted my existence,
precisely enough
to accommodate.
While joy erupted around you
like breeze across meadows,
I remained tethered to glowing pixels,
shouldering the burden
of aspirations we'd once shared
through endless twilights
and weary dawns.

Eventually,
came their dissatisfaction–
not for my actions,
but for what I couldn't provide
in their preferred manner.
And when criticism gathered,
you never inquired about my perspective.
You never positioned yourself as ally.
You merely requested
contrition.
Not for wrongdoing–
but for inadequacy
I couldn't remedy.
So I expressed regret.

Not from shame,
but from attachment.
Because somewhere,
I'd absorbed the lesson
that caring sometimes required
sacrificing yourself
for tranquility.

I remained motionless–
neither honored
nor acknowledged–
and delivered phrases
that burned during their exodus.
It transcended mere contrition.

It was my self-worth,
methodically unwrapped
and surrendered
to preserve delicate equilibrium
from collapse.

And you?
You observed.
You permitted it to dissolve
as though weightless.
That moment persists–
not thunderous,
not piercing–
but in the hidden chambers
I rarely explore.

A record
not of defeat,
but of everything
I relinquished
simply to suffice
for devotion
that never had to compromise.

While You Watched Me Break

I convinced myself,
this is devotion–
to yield,
to endure,
to swallow my inquiries
simply to preserve your universe intact.
Even during your departures.

Always accompanied by
the ally from your past,
who studied me like an intruder,
who privately ridiculed my form,
scorned my garments,
and wrapped her venom in grins.
I remained mute.

Not when you lingered beyond intentions,
fabricating justifications I struggled to accept.
Not when your absence spoke volumes
beyond any farewell.

You questioned why I couldn't mirror her.
You invited their poison into our sanctuary,
into our intimacy,
until I became the outsider
and they, the kinship.

They violated boundaries without permission—
claimed themselves essential,
while sowing suspicion like thorns
in what we were cultivating.
You witnessed the destruction.
And more devastating—
you weaponized it.
Transformed my tenderness into culpability,
my anguish into evidence
that I was the source of chaos.
I couldn't recognize it then.

I was too saturated with attachment,
too blinded by conviction
that you remained the person I'd wed.
That if I simply grasped more desperately,
you'd return to my embrace.

But devotion should never
demand erasing yourself
merely to qualify as sufficient.
And I—
I was beyond sufficient.
You simply refused to acknowledge it.

Not Even Your Truth

Because I requested your return
from distant obligations—
simply to our shared foundation,
to the emptiness I occupied
with anticipation—
you forged it into ammunition.

You and your circle
wielded my yearning like chains
to shackle me to shame.
Declared my hunger
was controlling.
Proclaimed my affection
exceeded limits.

You delivered them
the chronicle of my grief,
and they transformed it into narcissism.
Claimed I lacked dignity,
lacked courtesy—
even as I received them
into my domain
with swollen limbs, fevered flesh,
without protest.

I offered them comfort
while my own ribs

trembled with depletion.
Yet they departed
cataloging my inadequacies.
And you—
you trusted their verdict.
Crueler still—
you demanded I submit,
to collapse,
to express remorse once more.

That season—
December's frost was mild
beside your withdrawal.
You suggested
perhaps we should divide.
You termed it space.

I recognized it as retribution
for daring to possess limits.
That's when understanding struck—
I was never your priority.
Never your selection.
Never even your reality.
Despite bearing your name,
I ranked beneath her.

And I maintained silence.
I continued attempting faith
in the person I'd wed,
even though he'd already
abandoned the conversation.

Phase 6: Eclipse (The End)

The moon didn't fall–
it simply slipped behind a shadow
while I stood beneath it,
waiting for light that wouldn't return.
These are the poems from that fading–
when love dimmed without a sound,
and everything I believed
was gently eclipsed
by the ache of knowing it was over.

When You Let Go of "Us"

You announced,
Let's divide,
as though devotion were a portal
I had sealed
deliberately.
Yet I remained positioned
in the corridor,
expecting–
arms cradling tenderness
you'd ceased pursuing.

Behind you,
voices murmured,
framing stories
with confidence
only distance gives.
They read signs
that weren't there,
as if affection
was a flaw
when spoken too freely.
They said I was holding on
too tightly.
That "Mine"
on a phone screen
was possession,
not poetry.

But they weren't there
when I stood still
through the quiet shifts–
when your travels
became echo chambers
I could no longer enter.
They weren't there
when I swallowed
the unease
that settled like dust
on our shared spaces.
When I bent so far
to welcome comfort
you no longer offered.
Still,
they called me difficult.
Still,
you grew distant.
And for the simple act
of asking–
for presence,
for tenderness,
for time that felt ours–
I was told
to make amends
for emotions
I had no reason to hide.
I opened our home
with grace,
my voice gentler
than my wounds allowed.

I thought kindness
would carry us through.
But kindness
is easy to misunderstand
when hearts have already shifted.
And so,
you let others
describe me
in shapes I didn't recognize.
You nodded
at their stories
and looked at me
like I had become one.
That winter,
something in me
began to break.
Not loudly—
not in the way
things crash—
but like silence
that freezes a garden
overnight.
There was no fight,
no farewell worth remembering—
just a stillness
that cut deeper
than sound ever could.
And within that silence,
I discovered:
sometimes,
devotion doesn't conclude

with fury–
it concludes
with another person
casting the vote
on your behalf.

Fasting for Love

It began quietly–
not with words,
but with silence
that made its own noise.
There was an unspoken belief
that my sorrow was insecurity,
that my softness hurt
because of how I looked,
not how I was made to feel.
No one asked
what it meant
to sit in a room
and hear the shape of my body
become a topic,
tossed between casual sentences
and cooling tea.
I began to believe–
maybe if I changed,
the weight would lift
from your eyes,
from your voice
when you grew distant.
So I signed in
to a wellness center,
a quiet place for rest and repair.
I told myself
it was for healing.

But deep down,
I wanted to be enough–
for you,
for the world around you.
I chose fasting.
Days passed–
no food,
only breath,
discipline,
and the fragile echo
of love I was still chasing.
My body shrank,
my voice wavered,
but I waited.
Waited for a sign
of your nearness,
for presence to match care,
for warmth to visit
and not just pass through.
You came.
But only briefly.
A birthday visit,
your smile already looking forward
to someplace else.
To familiar hills
where laughter came easy.
That night,
a call came.
Faces lit by candles,
a cake held in hands not mine.
I smiled–

too tired to sit up,
too loyal to look away.
I asked for time.
Just a few more hours.
But asking made me
too much again.
The words floated back:
"Possessive."
"Emotional."
As if longing
were a crime of the heart.
I heard voices
off-screen–
soft on one side of the phone,
sharp on the other.
The kind that say,
"She's always upset,"
while planning another
beautiful escape.
And I lay there,
weak from hunger,
holding their absence
like a second skin.
No one asked
how I was healing.
No one asked
if I was human
beneath the effort
to become lighter,
quieter,
less.

I don't wonder what kind of people
could celebrate joy
beside someone's struggle.
But I still ask–
what kind of love
leaves a quiet room
and never turns back?
Even then,
I didn't speak.
Because silence,
I had learned,
hurt less than the cost of truth.
Would anyone else
accept this?
Lying in a narrow bed,
body trembling,
while the world continued
without pause?
I was not them.
And perhaps,
you were never mine
in the way I was yours.
Something broke that day–
not just the body,
but the part of me
that still believed
love always returns.
I was hungry–
for food,
for time,
for the soft presence

I'd once given
without asking.
And when the bills arrived,
I reached for my mother–
not only for help,
but for the strength
to survive
what wasn't there anymore.
You gave me silence,
and the memory of a song
sung somewhere else–
a tune that floated louder
than the apology
that never came.

The Day the Pot Was Shattered

You began to find flaws
where once you found warmth.
My words became weapons,
my quiet—a battlefield.
Even the air between us
felt sharp with suspicion.

I remember the car rides—
once filled with music and laughter,
your fingers tapping gently on mine,
roads unfolding like promises.
Now they held only silence.
I stared at my lap,
trying not to breathe too loud,
agreeing with every word
like a student desperate
not to be sent away.

You asked for an apology.
Not for you—
for that, I would've offered
every breath,
every knee-bent moment,
without shame.

But this one was different.
It wasn't mine to give.
It was borrowed guilt—
wrapped in others' expectations,

bound in ribbons of pride
that were never mine to untie.

I said,
"Let me heal first."
But my need for space
was heard as defiance.
You rewrote the story–
called my sorrow selfish,
my boundaries betrayal.

And then–
like a door slammed in a storm–
you said, "We're done."
Just like that.

You left me
outside the life we made,
in the cold shadow
of a once-shared dream.
No goodbye.
No pause.
Not even a look
at what we'd built
with our hands and hearts.

I thought of ending it–
not to punish,
but to escape
the ache that filled my lungs
with every breath.

I stood at the edge—
of reason,
of existence—
whispering to something
only I could hear.
And somehow,
in that blackness,
something answered.

Maybe it was memory.
Maybe it was the echo
of the person I used to be—
the one who loved wildly
without asking
for anything in return.

You walked away.
But I remained—
not in that place,
but in life.

And now,
I sift through the fragments
of what we once held,
trying to hold
what's left of myself.

Because even broken,
even burnt,
even cast out—
a part of me still knows
what it meant
to love like that.

So fully.
So purely.
So much
that I nearly lost
everything.

The Night I Came Home

It was past midnight–
the world asleep,
but not the storm inside me.
A car door shut too softly,
like the closing of a chapter
no one warned me was ending.
No words of farewell,
just silence
pressed into the skin of goodbye.

A woman waited in the car–
cold eyes behind glass–
not a step forward,
not a nod of courtesy.
Just witness to the unravelling,
but never the weight of it.

My mother opened the door
with a thousand questions
she did not ask.
Her hands trembled,
but her lips stayed still–
for me.
She swallowed her sorrow
like medicine,
like love does
when it needs to be strong

No paternal presence.
No sibling.
No voice to ascend for me.
Only the reverberation of the man
who once vowed permanence
yet couldn't provide
justification,
a phrase,
a glance that lingered.

I positioned myself in the boundary
of the existence I had constructed
and the one I presently returned to—
not shattered,
yet stripped of the delusion
that devotion alone could suffice.

And still,
I waited by the window for days,
believing it was a storm,
not an ending.
believing it was turbulence,
not conclusion.
Because once,
Because once,
he held my hand
like I was the home
he never wanted to leave.

The Letter That Ended the Moon

I was the kind of woman
who would have walked barefoot
across the shards of his silence–
if it meant he'd just open the door again.
I would have washed the feet
of strangers who stood between us–
not even his kin,
just the ones he feared disappointing
more than losing me.

I was wedded to forever.
I dreamed of hands intertwined through decades,
of silver hair and shared pillows,
of love that wouldn't falter under fire.
But I watched the man I cherished
weaponize his voice–
declaring *mutual or I'll destroy you.*
He who once whispered "mine"
now hurled ultimatums like they were devotion.
I couldn't fathom the words
spilling from the same mouth
that once kissed my forehead
like I was sanctuary.

And then–
silence.
Not the mending kind.

The kind that erects walls
no contrition can scale.
He wouldn't emerge from his room.
Wouldn't face me.
Wouldn't speak.
Instead—
a letter.
Folded crisp like closure.
A word I never believed
would arrive on parchment.
He who scorned all faith
wielded it to sever me.
Three syllables
that obliterated everything
I was still desperately clutching.
My mother anchored beside me
every hour she could steal—
terrified that if she departed,
I'd surrender to the abyss
devouring me whole.
I couldn't swallow.
I couldn't rest.
I ached to call him—
just to confirm he remained human,
that this wasn't mere nightmare
with my name scrawled in disappearing ink.
But he had vanished.
Vanished from my world,
yet not from the wound.
He abandoned unpaid prayers,
financial scars

I never acknowledged,
and a hollowness
that thundered louder
than his presence ever had.
I believed I wouldn't endure that day.
But perhaps my mother's murmured prayers
drowned out the sorrow.
Perhaps the universe
cradled me in its palm
just before I released my grip.
Perhaps the eclipse
wasn't the death of the sun–
just proof
that even radiance
must sometimes traverse shadow.
And here I stand.
Still breathing.
Not mended,
but whole enough to commence.

PHASE 7: PALE RISE (THE REBIRTH)

The moon didn't break–
it rose, pale and steady,
carrying scars like silver medals.
It didn't wait for apologies,
for explanations,
for anyone to come back and make it whole.
And neither did I.
This is the part after the ending–
where grief sharpens into grit,
and every breath becomes a rebellion.
These poems were written
with a spine rebuilt from silence,
from nights I thought I wouldn't survive.
But I did.
And like the moon,
I rose anyway.

The First Meal

I hadn't eaten in days.
Grief had carved a chasm so deep,
even water felt too weighty to swallow.
The plate sat there,
like an indictment.
Rice, steaming.
Lentils, quivering.
And my hands–
too weary to cradle anything but anguish.

They urged
"eat something."
As if betrayal didn't transform your throat
into a barricaded door.
As if the man I treasured
for six faithful years
hadn't disappeared behind malice so keen,
I mistook it for some hellish dream
I hadn't surfaced from yet.

Sleepless nights
coiled around me like shackles.
My tears refused to cease–
they only shifted form.
They seeped into my pillow,
into office chairs,
into crowded spaces
where I stood isolated
with no one comprehending

how profoundly I was fracturing
in chambers too hidden to witness.

He departed.
Not with remorse—
but with menace.
Without a flicker of compassion.
Without explaining
the existence he incinerated.
And I remained, charred and trembling,
with no words left
for what had been inflicted upon me.

But that day—
the day I lifted the spoon—
I accomplished something courageous.
Not thunderous,
but alive.

I nourished myself.
Not merely with sustenance,
but with the tiniest ember of faith:
that perhaps,
against all odds,
this torment wouldn't endure eternally.

No One Came

I whispered to the universe,
begging it to bend his heart back to me.
Lit candles. Held my breath.
Believed in signs that weren't there.
How could someone who once held my soul
just vanish, without goodbye,
without even flinching?

I tried to hate him.
I tried to call his silence cruelty.
But my heart, stubborn and bruised,
kept searching his name
in every quiet room,
kept hoping the door would open
and I'd see him standing there,
apology in hand, love in his eyes.

But no one came.

Not him.
Not the people I stood up for.
Not the ones who had watched me
pour my life into his.
Not a single hand
reached into the dark I was drowning in.

I cried through mornings,
hid tears behind work calls,
felt invisible in crowded rooms.
Even the black cars on the street

pulled at memories I couldn't unsee—
triggers dressed in leather seats
and echoes of a life
I thought would never leave me.

I was told healing would hurt.
That it might take years.
And I believed it—because the ache
had carved itself into my bones.

So I chose therapy.
I chose walking,
and breathing,
and talking to people who saw my pain
and didn't flinch.

I packed my wounds
and travelled with them—
to cities that didn't know my name,
to places where I could grieve
without being called dramatic.

And there, slowly,
I met a version of me
who didn't beg to be chosen.
Who didn't need apologies
to begin again.
Who learned
that healing isn't forgetting—
it's remembering without breaking.

No one came.
But I did.
For myself.
And that… was everything.

Inheritance

She never declared, "Be strong."
She simply stood–
while I crumbled at her feet,
on the floor she once swept with the burden of her own sorrow.

When the man I trusted vanished,
when food turned to ash and slumber fled,
when I pressed my ribs just to keep breathing
through a heartbreak I hadn't earned–
she didn't weep beside me.
She remained still.
Still like a mountain.
And somehow, that sufficed.

She knew anguish–
cradled it in her arms
when her child's laughter was severed too soon,
when her husband abandoned her
leaving behind three small daughters,
no resources,
no schooling,
and no luxury to collapse.

But she never fractured.
She ascended like she always had–
quietly,
completely,
blazing within.

And when I murmured,
"I don't know how to exist without him,"
she cupped my face–
that same hand that once braided my hair,
cooled my fevered brow,
held the cosmos together with tenderness–
and spoke:

"I endured with empty palms.
You possess enough to rebuild.
You're not shattered–
you're blossoming."

She didn't curse the heavens.
She didn't demand retribution.
She only gazed at me,
and with a voice forged from tempests and survival,
declared:

"Your tears hold weight.
A mother never forgets them–
and neither does the sky.
What wounded you will answer one day."

She didn't sermonize with words.
She guided with endurance.
She showed me
that being a woman isn't about how much you can bear–
but how high you can soar
when no one believes you will.

It's not about silence.
It's about strength born in stillness.
It's about kindling your own flame
when the world turns away.

And so I ascend–
not merely for myself,
but for her,
and every woman
who once thought she'd never stand
and still did.

You Thought I'd Stay There

I don't recall the precise moment
when sorrow stopped masquerading as love–
only that I finally ceased waiting
for an echo from a door long sealed.

There were days I contorted so far
just to preserve the calm
that I forgot I possessed a backbone.
And still, I gave–
time, tenderness,
even the fragments I required
to reconstruct myself.

I stood behind decisions
that were never mine to claim,
scorched my fingers
on the warmth I mistook for affection.
But no one returned
with balm when I ignited.

Yes, the silence was vicious.
Yes, the disappearance wounded.
Yes, it felt like treachery
wearing the face I once cherished.

But I've ascended from worse.
And even now,
Black cars and familiar melodies
can still bruise the day.

But they don't possess it.
Not anymore.

I've navigated through the debris
with nothing but a name
and a pulse.
I've mended myself
without requiring a mirror
to remind me who I am.

The truth is–
I was never destined to remain fractured.
Not for someone else's ease.
Not in the name of devotion
that was never reciprocated.

I may have loved fiercely,
but I live fiercer.
And that
is the chasm between
who I was then
and who I am now.

Let the past murmur if it wishes–
I don't belong to it anymore.

The Moon Didn't Wait

Not every silence is surrender.
Not every stillness means someone remained shattered.
They abandoned wreckage–
words like daggers, absence like wildfire,
and the kind of quiet that coils around your ribs
until breathing forgets how to be tender.

They averted their gaze as tears transformed into ink,
as heartbreak folded itself into letters
never destined to be sent.

But the moon didn't wait for apologies or
explanations.
It kept ascending–
pulling tides, pulling strength, pulling me.

I ascended too–
not with clamor, but with certainty.
Not to be witnessed, but to be complete.

Where they expected me to wither, I flourished.
Not in the light they stole,
but in the darkness they abandoned.

I rose–
not in fury,
but in something profounder.
In dignity.
In truth.

In a strength that didn't require proclamation,
only embodiment.

They spoke of devotion
while wielding my loyalty like a ladder.
They praised my flame
until it illuminated rooms they couldn't command.
And when I ceased dimming myself,
they declared it excessive.

I once believed love meant surrendering
without tallying the cost.
But authentic love doesn't
demand you vanish for its ease.

So I stopped asking why they departed.
Why they transformed.
Why the burden was never distributed.
Some questions don't require answers—
they require departures.

I descend from women
who weathered tempests with fractured hands
and tearless eyes.
Who interred dreams
and still sowed seeds
the following dawn.
My mother didn't sermonize strength—
she embodied it.

And so did I.

Not all conclusions arrive with warnings.
Sometimes, they come with mirrors.

And the most arduous thing you'll ever do
is gaze into one
and choose yourself.

But I did.
I am no longer grieving
the version of me that remained mute.
She fulfilled her purpose.
Now, I inscribe in her honor—
so no woman forgets her value.

Let them label me obstinate,
frigid, indifferent.
They don't comprehend
what it demands to endure
without resentment.

Even the moon—
scarred and sacred—
didn't wait for those
who couldn't match her radiance.

She rose anyway.
And so did I.

Phase 8: Blood Moon (The Reveal)

The darkness didn't return–
it burned red,
casting truth on every shadow
they thought would stay hidden.
Lies glimmered under its glow,
betrayals stood where they were sown.
No mask survived this light.
This is the moment after the end–
when the quiet gathers its evidence
and the night delivers it back.
These poems were written
in the heat of revelation,
where karma takes attendance
and no one walks away unseen

Blackboard of Betrayal

They called him gentle-
a man of principles:
truth, accountability, justice.
He smiled like a savior,
spoke like a prophet,
loved in lines rehearsed to perfection.

But behind closed doors
lay chapters never read in any classroom.
Hidden debts and borrowed names,
purchases made with another's trust.
Signatures offered in faith turned into weapons.

She was painted the affliction.
Her devotion dismissed as
nothing more than inconvenience.

He spoke to many of technicalities and loopholes—
that certain bonds were discussed but wisely avoided.
Yet now, he clings to whatever law serves him,
twisting it to crush the one he vowed to protect.

Irony sharpened into malice.
He laughed with those who whispered against her—
mocking her choices, her pain.
Fear was his veil. Rage, his armor.
And when discomfort grew,

he erased his own blood as if family
were ink easily scrubbed from a page.
Those who raised him--discarded.

No confrontation, just silent deletion.
A mirror held up, then smashed
before truth could stare back.
The lies travel faster than healing,
filling rooms where truth cannot breathe.
And while he plays the victim,
he dismantles a home with calculated precision.

Love didn't abandon him-- he walked away,
wearing righteousness never earned.
And somewhere, lessons are still taught by those
who never learned them.

What lesson is that?
To wear virtue as costume?
To silence those who bled for you?
To build your life on borrowed loyalty and betrayed
trust?
There is no curriculum for cruelty disguised as control.
No syllabus for unmaking a soul.
But karma--
she never misses an examination.
And time--
grades in silence.

The Architect of Illusion

In daylight, he was cathedral music—
all soaring notes and sacred harmonies,
a man who inquired after your mother's arthritis,
who knew which nephew graduated college,
who spoke of virtue like he'd authored scripture.
But behind closed doors,
he became editor of your reality.
Affection arrived with invoices.
Tenderness required receipts.
Every gesture of love
came stamped with conditions
written in disappearing ink.

He studied your vulnerabilities
like a cartographer mapping continent—
memorizing each fault line,
each place where you might crack
under precisely applied pressure.

Your dreams became his mirrors,
reflected back so perfectly
you forgot who dreamed them first.
He fed you slivers of hope—
just enough to sustain your hunger,
never enough to nourish your soul.

When exhaustion claimed you,
he gifted blame wrapped in sympathy,
his voice honeyed with false mercy:

"If only you tried harder.
If only you understood."

Then he'd emerge into the world
draped in your sacrifices,
wearing your sleepless nights
like badges of his patience,
your tears as testimony
to his sainthood.

The congregation saw his halo.
I knew the hands that forged it.

This wasn't love—
it was alchemy in reverse,
turning gold to lead,
light to shadow,
truth to something
that bent until it broke.

In those suffocating hours,
reality became clay in his hands—
molded, reshaped, fired
until you questioned
the sound of your own heartbeat,
the memory of your own name.

The audience still rises
for his standing ovations.
But I have seen the rehearsals—
the broken props,
the discarded scripts,

the understudies
who never made it to morning.

They worship his light.
But shadows remember
their makers.

And I–
I am the archive
of his darkness.

Queen of Sins

She anoints herself in drugstore divinity,
each stroke of lipstick
a prayer to the altar of her own making.
In mirrors she finds congregation–
the lone worshipper
of a goddess born from vanity.

She adopts sons she never labored to bear,
collects their futures
like gemstones in her counterfeit crown,
each dream she hoards
a trophy of quiet theft.
Every trip becomes her dominion,
every threshold crossed an act of conquest.

She colonizes bedrooms with her presence,
pushes rightful voices into the shadows,
settles into spaces
built from other women's sacrifice.
The young bride is sent to tend the elders,
while she swathes herself in borrowed reverence,
turning kindness into currency,
love into leverage.

Daylight exposes her dependence–
this queen who cannot rule her own solitude.
She clings to masculine hands

like a drowning woman,
never counting the bonds she severs
to secure her grip.
In staged moments
she performs a maternal pantomime,
gestures that blur lines that should remain sacred,
stirring waters that should never have been disturbed.

She prescribes ruin
with the certainty of the unhealed,
her spineless ally nodding along—
thoughts that flow only from her poisoned well.

Yet the show continues.
To the outside world
her kingdom glitters flawless,
her name is sung like blessing.
But beneath the gold leaf,
the palace floor is sticky
with the wine of stolen joy,
its corridors haunted
by the cries of lives she rearranged.

Karma will not roar like thunder—
it will seep in quietly,
like water through stone,
cracking the mirrors she worships,
stripping the crown from her head.
And when the masks fall,
she will stand unadorned

before the truth she fled from–
a hollow queen
drinking from the chalice
she once filled for others.

The Final Lesson

Some souls are born with cathedral hearts–
vast enough to shelter strangers,
to transform enemies into family
through sheer force of believing.

She was an architect of belonging,
building bridges where others saw chasms,
offering her table to those
who had never learned to set one.

Others entered her sacred geometry
not as invader but as invited–
folded into the fabric of her days
like thread woven into gold.

But hospitality, when unlimited,
becomes the blueprint for destruction.

She carved space from her own life–
holidays hollowed out for their comfort,
bedrooms surrendered to their presence,
intimate moments diluted
by an audience she never requested.

Privacy became currency
she spent without counting the cost,
silence shared like communion bread
until nothing remained her own.

And for this generosity of spirit,
they named her jealous–

as if a bride could pause her rapture
on her wedding day
to envy applause from the gallery.

They mistook her open hands
for grasping fingers,
her devotion for possession,
her love for something
that needed their permission to exist.

She became their constellation–
nurse, maid, teacher, keeper
of their borrowed family's flame.
She cooked their comfort,
shared their journeys,
tutored through midnight hours
pouring herself out
like wine from an endless chalice.

When exhaustion claimed her,
they branded her "excessive."
When illness made her fragile,
they called her brokenness toxic.

And when her marriage shattered–
when the very foundation
she'd built with bleeding hands
crumbled beneath betrayal–
they offered nothing
but the echo of their absence.

Yet somehow they found appetite
for holidays with the man

who'd abandoned her altar.
They whispered counsel
into ears that once heard her prayers,
teaching him the art
of discarding devoted hearts.

They didn't merely witness destruction—
they authored it,
pulling threads
until her tapestry unraveled,
then claiming the chaos
as natural disaster.

But they underestimated
the alchemy of a woman
who gives with open palms
and learns to rise
with clenched fists.

Yes, they feast now
on the ruins of her generosity,
sharing the spoils
of a life they helped dismantle,
calling their cruelty destiny,
their betrayal progress.

As if truth were something
to be buried beneath
carpets woven from deception.

But justice keeps longer records
than comfort allows,

and karma requires no invitation—
only patience.

One day, when their children
reach for love with tender hands,
may they never encounter
such sweetly poisoned embrace.
May they never learn that
family can be the cruelest fiction

Because this devastation
was no accident of fate—
it was architecture,
carefully planned,
methodically executed.

They took a quiet life
and broke it thunderously,
rewrote a sacred covenant
as if hearts were rough drafts
awaiting their editorial hand.

But the woman they discarded
did not dissolve into grief.
She rose from heartbreak
like phoenix from pyre—

Not to return
to the scene of her burning,
but to remember
the fire they lit
and the wings it gave her.

Let them celebrate their victory.
She calls it transformation.

Let them keep what they stole.
She has learned
to build kingdoms
from ash.

Epilogue

She spoke to the moon – because it never interrupted.
This book is woven from silence and flame.
Each poem, a wound that learned to sing.
Each chapter, a lunar phase –
waning, vanishing, ascending again.

I did not bleed these words to destroy reputations
or point accusatory fingers.
I wrote them to resurrect myself.

To cast light into corners
where I once wept in shadows.
To alchemize anguish into art.
And above all, to cease apologizing
for the woman forged in abandonment.

The moon has always been my witness.
She observed the nights I suffocated on sorrow.
She heard the names I howled into fabric.
She remained silent – not from indifference,
but to cradle me tenderly
when no human hands would.

And eventually, she whispered this truth:
even when fractured, the moon never pleads
with the sky for permanence.
She disappears, she mends, she emerges –
fuller, gentler, inexorable.

So I became her apprentice.

To those who shattered me –
you provided the cinders.
But I kindled the fire.

To those who exploited, muted, obliterated me –
you revealed who I refuse to become.

To those who loved me authentically –
your radiance carried me home.

And to you, reader –
if you've ever felt diminished, discarded, invisible –
may this book embrace your spirit like moonbeams.
Gentle but undeniable.

Because healing doesn't always roar.
Sometimes, it illuminates.

And when it does –
no force can extinguish that light from you again.

Thank You

To my mother –
who stayed when the world walked away,
whose silent strength became my blueprint for rising.

To my sisters –
one who walks beside me still,
one who watches from beyond the stars.
Both carried pieces of my heart
through the darkest seasons.

To the elders who heard me
with the tenderness of parents,
who gave their time like love,
treating my pain as if it were
their own daughter's tears.

To every woman who has ever
loved too deeply,
given too freely,
trusted too completely –
this book is our shared testimony
that breaking does not mean broken.

To the moon, my constant companion –
thank you for witnessing
what others chose not to see,

for holding space in the darkness,
and for teaching me
that light always returns.

To those who betrayed me –
your cruelty became my curriculum.
Your absence showed me
the strength I never knew I had.

To my readers –
thank you for holding these words,
for seeing light in the darkness,
for understanding that healing
sometimes speaks in poetry.

And finally, to myself –
for refusing to disappear
when disappearing felt easier,
for choosing the pen over silence,
for learning that my voice
was worth saving.

Thank you all for being part
of this resurrection.